The Boxcar Children investigate legendary creatures!

"Elf rock? What's that?" asked Violet. She had not had much time to learn about the creatures they'd come to Iceland to investigate.

"That is where elves are said to live—in the stones," said Dr. Iris.

"Like an elf guesthouse?" Benny said. "Will we get to see them?"

"Remember, Benny, we talked about that," Jessie said. "The elves in Iceland are said to be mostly invisible. That's why they are also called the *huldufólk*, or 'hidden people.' We might not actually see one, even if they do exist."

"I remember," Benny said. "But you said 'mostly invisible.' If we're careful, we might just sneak up on one!"

THE BOXCAR CHILDREN®

CREATED BY
GERTRUDE CHANDLER WARNER

CREATURES OF LEGEND

BOOK 2

MYSTERY OF
THE HIDDEN ELVES

ALBERT WHITMAN & COMPANY
CHICAGO, ILLINOIS

Copyright © 2021 by Albert Whitman & Company
First published in the United States of America
in 2021 by Albert Whitman & Company

ISBN 978-0-8075-0805-3 (hardcover)
ISBN 978-0-8075-0814-5 (paperback)
ISBN 978-0-8075-0809-1 (ebook)

Printed in the United States of America
10 9 8 7 6 5 4 3 2 1 LB 24 23 22 21 20

Illustrations by Thomas Girard

Visit The Boxcar Children® online at www.boxcarchildren.com.
For more information about Albert Whitman & Company,
visit our website at www.albertwhitman.com.

CONTENTS

AT THE TOP
OF THE WORLD

L and ho!" Benny Alden called, pointing out the window of the airplane. For hours, he had seen only the white waves of the ocean far below. Now, as he pressed his nose up to the window, a green island rose up in the distance.

"It just comes right up out of the water," Jessie said, peering past her brother.

Ten-year-old Violet had been napping in the row behind Benny and Jessie. She rubbed her eyes. "It's so green. I thought Iceland would be more…icy."

Henry looked up from the guidebook he was reading. At fourteen, he was the oldest of the Alden children and had learned about Iceland in geography. "Greenland is the icier one. It's even farther north than Iceland."

Benny tilted his head. "So Greenland is icier, and Iceland is greener? That's confusing."

Henry laughed. "I agree. But Iceland can get icy too, especially in the winter."

"Well, it's a good thing we're visiting in the middle of the summer," Violet said. "I hope we get perfect weather. I want to take lots of pictures."

The pilot came over the speaker to announce they were starting their descent. As the plane turned, the children got an even better view of the coast. In the distance, they could see white-tipped mountains. It had been a long flight, but their destination was already worth the wait.

Then something caught Jessie's eye. At first she thought it was a storm cloud over the mountains. But when they got closer, she saw that it looked more like smoke. Jessie was twelve. She liked to be prepared when she and her brothers and sister traveled. "Excuse me," she said as a flight attendant walked past, checking seat belts. "Is there a wildfire going on?"

The flight attendant shook her head and spoke calmly. "The smoke you see is coming from a volcano. Iceland has about thirty active volcanoes."

"Thirty!" Benny stuck his nose up to the window. "Is there hot lava everywhere?"

Violet did not like the sound of that.

The flight attendant gave a gentle smile. "No need to worry. With so many volcanoes, we get some activity about every five years, but it is not like the pictures you see of hot lava and fire."

"I'd like to see a volcano close up someday," Jessie said. "Just not on this trip."

"So they aren't dangerous?" Violet asked.

"The biggest danger is from ashfall," the flight attendant said. "It can make it hard to breathe, and if the heat melts the ice, then we worry about flooding.

But we have many scientists who monitor them. They'll tell us when we need to be more careful." She smiled. "We're almost ready to land. Please stay in your seats until all the other passengers get off. I will take you to meet someone who will take you to meet your party."

After the flight attendant left, Violet said, "If that volcano erupts, the scientists who are watching it can't stop it."

"Dr. Iris will tell us if it's a problem," said Henry. Dr. Iris was a friend of Grandfather's. She was a paleontologist, but she also had another job: investigating unsolved mysteries around the world. She was planning a television program for children about the mysteries. The Aldens had met her at summer camp, where there was said to be a bigfoot lurking in the forest. The children were so helpful in figuring out what was going on that Dr. Iris had asked them to come along as she investigated other reports of legendary creatures.

Jessie got out a small journal. "I'm going to write down that we saw a volcano. Dr. Iris said she wants to know everything that interests us, so she'll know what to talk about when she films the program."

"I hope this trip doesn't have as many scary things happen as the last time we were with Dr. Iris," Violet said. She loved going on adventures and traveling. But sometimes the legends of creatures worried her, even if she was pretty sure they weren't real.

"I see the airport!" Benny bounced up and down in his seat. "We're almost there!"

After the plane landed, the friendly flight attendant introduced the children to another airline worker, who led them to customs. As they walked, the man asked, "Is this your first time in Iceland?"

"Yes. We're going to go look for legendary creatures!" Benny told him.

The man laughed. "I hear that from many visitors," he said. "But I hope you take the time to enjoy the beautiful landscape, too, all the waterfalls and mountains."

Violet was glad the man did not seem worried about their mission—or the volcano.

With the man's help, it didn't take long for the children to get through customs. Just beyond was a big crowd waiting for passengers.

"There's Dr. Iris!" Benny pointed to a woman with silvery-black hair who was waving at them. The children thanked the airline attendant and headed off to meet her.

"Hello!" Dr. Iris said when they reached her. She gave each of them a hug. "Are you ready for our adventure?"

"We still get to go?" Benny asked.

"We saw smoke from a volcano," Violet said. "We were afraid our trip would be canceled."

"So far, the eruption is not a problem," Dr. Iris said. "But we will listen to the news, and I'll keep your grandfather updated with all of the information we have. Now, we have a lot to do. Let's get your bags and start investigating!"

Once they had their luggage, the Aldens followed Dr. Iris out of the terminal. As soon as they were outside, a blast of cold wind hit them.

"Brrr. I'm glad you told us to bring warm clothes," Jessie said to Dr. Iris.

"Yes, the weather in Iceland can be more extreme than people think, even in the summertime. Our car is over this way. I've rented a vehicle that can take us over some of the rough roads on our route. We're going to do some real exploration. And I'll introduce you to Todd. He's a cameraman who is going to take some footage of our trip."

"Are we going to be on camera for the show?" Benny asked. He straightened up and puffed out his chest.

Dr. Iris smiled. "The show will be put together later on, in a studio. Todd is here to get some on-site footage, but you might find your way into a shot or two." She winked. "Where is Todd anyway? I told him to wait here."

"Is that him?" Henry pointed at a man with a beard. He was lying on the pavement across the parking lot, taking pictures of the bumper of an old car.

"Todd!" Dr. Iris called. "I've collected the Aldens. We should go."

"Almost finished," the man yelled, snapping a few more photos. Then he leaped up and almost tripped over his shoelaces on his way over.

"This is Todd," Dr. Iris said. She introduced the children.

"You didn't say some of them would be little kids," the cameraman said, staring down at Benny. "I've never done a job with kids along. How old are you anyway?"

"I'm six," Benny said, frowning. "That's not so little. Your shoe is untied."

Todd looked down at his shoe and blushed. "Right," he said, bending down to tie his laces.

"The Aldens are very capable," Dr. Iris said. "And as you can see, they have a very good eye for spotting details. They will be a big help in making our show perfect for children."

"Why were you taking a picture of that old car?" Violet asked. "Was it for the show?"

"No, of course not," Todd scoffed. "I don't just take film. I do still photography, too, and I have a gallery show coming up. The way the light was reflecting off that car's bumper made a great photo."

Violet tilted her head. She didn't see it.

"Let's get the luggage loaded," Dr. Iris said. "We have a bit of a drive before we reach our guesthouse."

Benny looked up at the sky. "Why is it light out?" he said. "I thought it was going to be night here when we landed."

"We've come to Iceland at just the right time," Dr. Iris said. "We're so far north, you'll get to see the last few days of what's called the midnight sun."

"How can you see the sun at midnight?" Benny asked. "First, I learned that Iceland is green instead of icy. And now it's sunny at night? I think this place should be called Opposite Land."

Dr. Iris laughed. "Those are very good observations, Benny. I might just discuss them at the beginning of the television show. Does anyone else know why the midnight sun occurs?"

"I might," Jessie said. She had learned about the planets and the sun in science class. "The earth is like a ball, but it's tilted as it goes around the sun." She put her hands together to make the shape of a ball tilted to one side. "Benny, if you stand still, you can be the sun, and I'll be the earth." She walked partway around Benny and stopped. "See how the top of my hands are tilted toward you now?"

"Yes," Benny said.

"That means it's summer. We're so far north that we still see the sun over the top of the earth, even when we're turned away from it during the night. Do you get it?"

"I do," Violet said.

"I think I do." Benny didn't sound so sure.

"That's okay," Jessie said. "Just remember we're much farther north on the earth when we are in Iceland compared to being at home."

"Yes, that's a good thing to remember," said Dr. Iris. "Where you are on the planet matters for all sorts of things: weather, light, the plants and animals around you. It also affects the stories people tell. We'll see if it has something to do with what we've come to investigate."

"The legend of the hidden elves!" said Benny.

"That's right," Dr. Iris said. "Let's get started."

CHAPTER 2

THE HOUSE OF ELVES

It's so pretty," Violet said as the Aldens rode along a narrow road. To the left, rocky cliffs stretched down to the ocean. In the distance to the right, mountains reached up and touched the clouds. "I'm used to seeing the ocean. And we've been to mountains. But I've never seen both at once."

The road wound its way along the coastline until it came to a town by a lake. The houses in the town were small and looked alike but with brightly colored roofs.

"The houses are different from home too," said Jessie. "They look cozy."

"That's one of my favorite parts of traveling," Dr. Iris said as she pulled into a gas station. "Seeing how other people live. I want to get gas now so we can get up and be on our way tomorrow."

Todd got out of the car along with Dr. Iris. "I need to get a shot of that sky. It's incredible," he said as he went around to the back to get a camera.

"I want to take a picture of it too," Violet said. She took her own camera out of her backpack. "It's such a pretty mix of pink and blue and yellow."

"Why does the sky look extra big here?" Benny asked.

Henry leaned forward and rested his arms on the seat in front of him. Even from inside the car, the sky did look bigger. "It seems like something is missing," Henry said. "But I don't know what…"

Outside, Todd walked into a nearby field. It was rockier than he'd expected. Todd nearly tripped over his shoelaces again but caught himself before he fell all the way down.

As he was kneeled down to tie his shoe, Todd reached out and placed something in his camera bag. Violet thought he had put his camera inside for safekeeping, but when Todd came back to the car, his camera was still his hands.

"Did you find something?" Violet asked.

Todd looked confused. Then he looked down at his camera bag and adjusted the flap. "Oh, that? I just had to change lenses."

Violet was going to point out that Todd had the same lens on his camera as before, but he hurried past her and placed his camera bag in the back of the car.

Before long, Dr. Iris came out of the station and joined the others in the car. "We shouldn't have to stop again until tomorrow night," she said as they started down the road.

After a few more miles, the car slowed down, and they pulled into a parking lot next to a white house with a red roof. The sign in front read *Greylag*

Goose Guesthouse. Underneath was a picture of a goose sitting next to a big rock.

Todd leaned out the window. "It's small," he said. He didn't sound happy. "I thought we'd be staying in hotels, with exercise rooms and swimming pools. This place doesn't look like it has anything extra."

"Guesthouses are common in Iceland," Dr. Iris said. "Not many people live in the countryside. But when summer comes, tourists come from around the world and need places to stay. We're lucky we made it before the summer rush."

"I think it looks perfect," said Jessie. "We don't need much."

"There's another reason I wanted to stay here," Dr. Iris said. "The owner knows a lot about the legends in Iceland, and there's a famous elf rock nearby."

"Elf rock? What's that?" asked Violet. She had not had much time to learn about the creatures they had come to Iceland to investigate.

"That is where elves are said to live—in the stones," Dr. Iris said.

16

"Like an elf guesthouse?" Benny said, getting out of the car. "Will we get to see them?"

"Remember, Benny, we talked about that," Jessie said. "The elves in Iceland are supposed to be mostly invisible. That's why they are also called the *huldufólk*, or 'hidden people.' I don't think you are going to see an actual elf, even if they do exist."

Benny sighed. "I remember. But you said 'mostly invisible.' Maybe I can sneak up on them."

"Maybe," Jessie said, rubbing her little brother's hair.

Violet gave a little shiver. "I'd rather not see them. Don't you think it's weird that there might be invisible creatures around?"

"I don't think they exist at all," Henry said. "So I'm not worried."

"This is exactly why I wanted the Aldens to come along!" Dr. Iris said to Todd. She was writing on a little notepad. "We need to get all different ideas about what children think about the legendary creatures of Iceland, so we know the best way to present them in the program."

A tall woman with long, white hair came out of the guesthouse. She was wearing a green dress with a hood on it. Violet thought the woman looked like an elf from the movies.

"Welcome to the Greylag Goose!" the woman called. She shook Dr. Iris's hand, and Dr. Iris introduced everyone.

"Call me Elin," the woman said. "I hope you are hungry. Dr. Iris and I decided on something special for your first night in Iceland. We're going to have a picnic under the midnight sun! How does that sound?"

"Great!" said Benny.

Henry chuckled. "Benny is happy to picnic anytime."

"Wonderful!" Elin continued. "We have some other guests who are going to join us, two families traveling together. You'll be able to meet some other children."

Elin showed the Aldens to their room. It looked very cozy. There were four beds, two on each side of the room, built against the walls.

The children put down their things and followed Elin out the back door onto a patio. Beyond it was a rocky field like the one they had seen at the gas station, but this time, some of the rocks were even taller than Benny.

"These don't look like the rocks at home," Jessie said. She reached out and touched one. "They are so rough. There are little holes in them."

"That's because these are igneous rocks," Dr. Iris explained. "Igneous rocks come from volcanoes. Almost all the rock in Iceland is igneous rock. That's how the island was formed. Little by little over a very long time, lava came out of the ground and cooled, forming rock. Some of these rocks are from volcanoes that erupted thousands or even millions of years ago."

"Look!" Benny cried. "That one has a door on it!" He knelt down to look at a waist-high rock. A tiny, yellow door was leaning up against it. "Why is it so small?"

"I read about this in the guidebook," said Henry. "It has to do with the elves, doesn't it?"

"That's right," said Elin. "Lava rocks didn't just help create Iceland; they are also said to be where the hidden people live. The door is just for decoration. According to legend, elves do not need doors to get into their homes."

Elin pointed to a large stone in a field behind the house. "Plus, the real elf rock is over there. And it has a very…interesting history."

"What kind of history?" Violet asked.

"A number of years ago, people tried to build a road through the field, so they used heavy equipment to move that big rock. Then things started going very wrong. Machines broke. The weather turned bad. Workers got sick."

"Do people think it was because of the stone?" asked Jessie.

Elin nodded. "In Iceland, elves are usually thought to be friendly. They peacefully do many of the same activities as humans. But when their world is disrupted by humans, they can get upset."

"Like if their house is moved away?" said Benny.

"That's right. So many things were going wrong, the construction managers finally decided to put the rock back. Instead of moving the elf rock, they moved the road."

Violet looked at the rocks around them. "How do you know if a rock is an elf rock?"

"You don't, unless you talk to the people who live around a particular site," Elin replied. "People like me are trying to document all the stories, so we can learn about specific rocks and make a list, but there are so many of them, our list is far from complete."

Dr. Iris was scribbling notes as Elin spoke. When she looked up, she said, "May we take a look?"

"Of course," Elin said. "And listen closely too. Some people claim they can hear the elves."

Before Elin was done speaking, Benny was running ahead.

"So much for sneaking up." Jessie laughed. The children followed along with Dr. Iris and Todd.

Benny circled the rock. "It's big," he said. "But I bet five of these could fit inside our boxcar. How can a bunch of elves live inside?"

"The stories say the elves do magic," Dr. Iris said. "They make the inside of the rock much bigger than it looks on the outside."

Benny reached out his hand, but Violet grabbed it. "Maybe we shouldn't touch it," she said. "I wouldn't like people standing around our house knocking on the walls."

"I don't want to just look at it," Benny said as he knelt down and put his ear close to the rock. "I want to listen. Can everybody be quiet?"

Everyone stopped talking. Jessie noticed Todd filming them. After a few moments, she asked, "Do you hear anything?"

"No." Benny stood back up. "Maybe the elves are sleeping."

"Speaking of sleeping," Dr. Iris said, checking her watch, "we'd better get our picnic underway before it gets too late."

Just then, Elin waved from the guesthouse and the children headed back. She introduced the Aldens to the other families who had arrived. There were three boys and two girls along with their parents. "My kitchen helper is still working on the picnic. While we're waiting, would you like to learn an old game the children play in Iceland?"

"Yes!" both Benny and one of the other boys said at once.

"I thought you might. The game is called Thieving Elves," Elin said.

Violet clasped her hands together and looked out at the elf rock. "If there are elves in the rocks, can they hear us talk? Won't they get angry that we're pretending elves steal things? I know I wouldn't like it if someone said I was a thief."

"You're going to pretend to be elves who are taking things from rich dwarves," Elin said. "According to stories, dwarves are known to hoard their gold and not share it with anyone. So the elves like to teach them a lesson."

"There are dwarves in Iceland too?" Jessie asked.

"Iceland has many tales about all different kinds

of creatures," Elin said. "Elves and dwarves and trolls are just a few of them. One of you will be the dwarf, and the rest of you will be elves. Jessie, if you will get that chair over there, and, Violet, if you will get the bucket by the door, we can go out into the field, and I'll explain the rest."

Jessie and Violet and the others followed Elin to a spot by the rock, where Jessie set the chair down.

"Violet, why don't you show them what is in the bucket?"

Violet reached in and took out a wooden block.

"You're going to pretend these are blocks of gold," Elin said. "When the game starts, the dwarf closes their eyes and counts to fifteen. While they are counting, the elves run from their base and try to take something from the bucket. When the dwarf gets to fifteen, the elves freeze and put their hands behind their backs, like this." She took a block out of the bucket and put it behind her.

"Then the dwarf calls out one elf they think has stolen something. If your name is called and you are holding something, you have to put it back in the bucket. Then go back to the base. If your name isn't called, you get to keep the block and take it back to the base. You take turns playing the dwarf, so no one is it for too long. In the end, the elf with the most gold is the winner. Want to give it a try?"

Everyone was very excited to play. Todd took out his video camera. "This might make some good footage for our project," he said.

One of the girls turned out to be very fast, and through a few rounds, she had collected a pile of blocks.

"I can't get the right camera angle," Todd grumbled. "I need to be up higher."

During Henry's turn at being the dwarf, Violet had almost reached the bucket when she stopped suddenly. Todd had climbed up on top of the elf rock. "Maybe you should get down from there," she said, forgetting about the game.

Todd waved his hand. "Are you kidding? This is great footage!"

"But you are on top of the elf rock," Benny said,

stopping to look up at him. "Didn't you hear the stories?"

Todd lowered his camera. "Come on! What's the worst that could—whoa!"

He lost his balance and fell to the ground. But this time, it was not because his shoe was untied.

Everyone stopped playing the game and stood still.

"Do you feel that?" Benny asked. "The ground is shaking!"

STORIES FROM SOMEPLACE

Was that...an earthquake?" Henry asked.

For a moment, no one moved. Then Elin went to help Todd up. "It was," she said. "Nothing to worry about though. Small earthquakes are common here."

Dr. Iris could see that everyone was a little shaken up. "Why don't we have our picnic now?" she said. "I'm sure everything is ready."

Before long, the group was filling their plates and

chatting on the patio. Todd went back to filming, and the group seemed to forget about the earthquake. But as Violet ate her sandwich, she couldn't help but stare at the big rock. It seemed impossible, but had it had something to do with the earthquake?

A girl from one of the other families distracted her. "This is our last night here," the girl said. "We're flying out tomorrow, but I wish we were staying longer."

"Did you see any elves?" Benny asked.

"I thought I might have seen one," the girl said. "I saw something move behind a big rock."

"I think it was a fox," an older girl said. "We did see a few foxes on our trip."

"If elves in Iceland are invisible, why do people who have never seen them believe they exist?" Jessie asked Elin. "When we were trying to figure out if a bigfoot was near Dr. Iris's camp, we learned we needed evidence, like bones or teeth that didn't come from any other species. How did people here start to believe in elves in the first place?"

"And why do they live in rocks?" Violet asked.

The whole idea seemed strange to her.

"I can answer parts of those questions." Elin set down her plate and told them a story. "The people who first came to Iceland did so a thousand years ago, during what we call the Time of Settlement. The settlers came mostly from Norway, which is in northern Europe. Later, settlers came from other countries in that same region. They didn't just bring their possessions when they moved here; they brought their stories too. Many of those cultures have stories of elves and dwarves and trolls. Imagine if you left your home to move somewhere else. You'd still remember the stories you'd been told, and you'd continue to tell them in the new place, especially at a time when there would have been only a few books."

Jessie nodded. "That makes sense. You wouldn't just forget all the stories you knew."

"But what about elves living inside the rocks?" Benny asked.

"Look around. It might help answer the question,"

said Elin. "What don't you see that you would see where you live?"

At the gas station, Henry had noticed that the landscape looked different somehow. Now, as he looked around the field, he realized why. "Trees! There are no trees!"

"Yes," Elin said. "There are many, many trees in northern Europe, and in the stories told there, elves live in the forests. But Iceland has never had many trees, and the first settlers cut down what few were here, not understanding how hard it would be to grow more."

Jessie thought for a moment. "So their stories had to change," she said. "If elves didn't have forests to live in, they had to live somewhere else."

"And Iceland has a lot of rocks." Henry thought back to what Dr. Iris had told them in the car. "Where you are on the planet affects what kinds of stories people tell."

Benny looked a little disappointed. "Does that mean elves aren't real? That they are just stories?"

"All stories come from someplace, Benny." Elin

winked. "I just collect those stories. I'll leave the evidence collecting to the scientists."

"We'll have plenty of time to talk more about that on our trip," said Dr. Iris. She looked down at her empty plate. "This was all very good. I don't think any of us realized how hungry we were."

"I hope you saved some room," Elin said. "You still have to try our Icelandic dessert."

Elin went inside and came out with a tray of pies. Once the pies were cut, everyone took a piece.

"Is this blueberry?" Jessie asked.

"It is bilberry. They are like blueberries but smaller and darker," Elin explained. "Bilberries are one of the few fruits that grow naturally in Iceland. Because it's so rocky here, most of our food needs to be sent by ship from other countries. But not bilberries."

Benny loved blueberries. He couldn't imagine not having them. But when he took a bite of his pie, his eyes got big. "Can they send some of these to where we live?" he said.

Everyone laughed.

When the group had finished eating, the children thanked Elin and said good night to the other families. They were not used to staying up so late, but they had gotten lots of rest on the airplane ride, so they weren't too sleepy.

"I want to write everything down before I go to bed," Jessie said as she got out her journal.

Violet rummaged in her backpack. "I can't find my toothbrush. I know I packed it."

"It might have fallen out in the car when you got your camera," Henry said. "We can go look for it."

Outside, there was still some light in the sky to the west, but the parking lot seemed dark. Violet couldn't see the big rock from where she stood, but she could imagine it standing out in the field all by itself.

"Don't you think it's strange that there was an earthquake the first day we got here?" she asked.

"Remember? Elin said Iceland has a lot of earthquakes." Henry opened the back door and leaned in so he could look under the seat.

"I didn't like it," Violet answered. "Do you

remember what she said about the elves not wanting their homes disturbed?"

"Yes. Sorry, Violet, I don't see the toothbrush here."

"Well, isn't it a little strange that as soon as Todd climbed up on that rock, the earthquake happened?"

Henry shrugged. "I guess. But I think it was just a coincidence. Hey, I found it!" Henry reached under the seat and pulled out the toothbrush case.

"I guess you're right," said Violet. "I like Elin, but I'm going to be happy when we get away from that big rock."

Henry yawned and handed Violet the toothbrush. "Let's get some rest. I'm sure you'll feel better about things in the morning."

"I hope so," she said.

—

The next morning, Henry awoke to a noise outside. His brother and sisters were still sleeping, so he decided to go see what had caused it. As he came out the front door, Todd was turning into the parking lot in the rental car.

After he was parked, Todd jumped out and went around to the front. He seemed to be looking for something on the front of the car.

"What happened?" Henry asked.

"Not much of a dent," Todd said, pointing to a spot on the bumper. "It was the strangest thing. I was turning around, and a post seemed to come out of nowhere!"

Henry looked to where Todd was pointing. The dent was right in the middle of the bumper. Henry wondered how Todd couldn't see a post that was right in front of him. But he asked, "What were you doing out so early?"

"Taking some photos," Todd said. "I can't believe the sky here."

Just then, a squawking noise came from out in the field, where two large, gray birds were waddling around.

Todd got out one of his cameras. "I suppose I should film those. Iris says that kids like to see footage of wildlife, so we should include as much as we can in the program." He walked toward the birds. One of them turned around to face him. It raised its wings, and then, as Todd got closer, it began to squawk again.

"Todd," Henry called. "I don't think it wants to be filmed." He looked at the animal and then at the sign for the guesthouse with the bird painted on it. "That must be a graylag goose. Geese will chase you if they get upset."

"I'm not scared of a bird," Todd said. He kneeled down and took a few pictures.

All of a sudden, the goose squawked and flapped its wings. Then it charged right at Todd.

Todd was so startled, he fell backward. The goose kept coming at him.

"Hey! This way!" Henry yelled, waving his arms.

The goose was distracted for a moment, and that was long enough for Todd to get to his feet. The bird squawked once more but didn't charge at Todd again.

"We're leaving!" Todd said to it. He laughed. "I

got some footage at least and no injuries to show for it."

Dr. Iris's voice came from behind them. "I hope you don't regularly get close to wild creatures," she said to Todd. "Some will be far more dangerous than a goose."

Todd shrugged. "Sometimes you have to take chances to get a good shot."

"Just make sure you are a little more careful on the rest of the trip," Dr. Iris warned. "We won't be places where it will be easy to get to a doctor. Now, Elin says breakfast will be ready shortly. I'd like to get underway soon."

After a big breakfast, Elin came outside to see them off. "Where are you visiting today?" she asked.

Dr. Iris got out a map. "We're going this way to our next guesthouse," she said, tracing her finger along the map.

Elin frowned. "Are you sure you want to go that route?"

"Why not?" asked Benny. "Are there lots of hidden elves that way?"

"Most people see Iceland by driving on the Ring Road around the coast," Elin said. "Some of the roads through the center of the country are not paved. They can be very rough."

"We'll be okay," Dr. Iris said cheerfully. "There are some sites along the way I want to see, and it's better for our research if we can visit parts of Iceland that most tourists don't see. I've driven all over the world. It shouldn't be a problem."

"All right," Elin said, but the concerned look stayed on her face. "Be careful! I hope you come back to visit sometime. And please do keep up on news reports about the volcano eruption. The situation can change very suddenly."

"We will. Okay, everyone, climb in," Dr. Iris said. "We've got some fantastic places to see today!"

CHAPTER 4

SHAPES IN THE FOG

The Aldens waved as they pulled out of the parking lot. It didn't take long for them to get out of town and into the open countryside. Big, flat spaces stretched for miles around, with snowcapped mountains in the distance. As they got farther away from the coast, they drove into fog. Before long, they couldn't see the mountains any longer.

Dr. Iris slowed the car.

"It's like we're driving in a cloud," Jessie said.

"It's kind of spooky," Benny said.

Violet twisted around in the seat to look out the back window. She was glad to be getting away from the elf rock. But the fog made her nervous. "It feels like there is someone right behind us, but I don't see a car."

"How can you feel someone behind you, especially when you are in a car?" Todd asked.

"I don't know. I just do. It's a feeling."

Todd made a snorting sound. "Kids! You're just imagining things."

"Let's talk about our work here," Dr. Iris said. "I hope we collect quite a bit of information today. We should go over what we've already learned. Would one of you take notes?"

"I will," Jessie volunteered, taking out her journal.

"Who wants to start?" Dr. Iris asked.

"The elves live in rocks," Benny said. "And they are invisible. Mostly. Except sometimes you can sneak up on them."

"They can get upset if their homes are disrupted," Violet added.

"Stories about elves and other creatures were brought here by the original settlers," Jessie said, "who came from countries where there were forests. Since there weren't forests here, the stories changed to fit the country."

"Good," Dr. Iris said.

"But what about proof?" Henry asked. "It will be hard to prove that they do exist. Because they're hidden, it's hard to know what might be caused by them and what isn't."

"We'll have to be extra sneaky," said Benny. "Then we might see one."

"That's right, Benny," said Dr. Iris. "Who knows what we might find? But in the meantime, we want to understand what some people in Iceland believe about the legends of these creatures. For example, when you say the word *elf*, people have many different images of what that is. Benny, how would you describe an elf?"

"Santa's helpers!" Benny said. "Short people with pointed ears."

"Yes, that's a common belief," Dr. Iris said.

"I watched a movie where the elves looked like us except they had pointed ears and some of them had blue and pink hair," Violet said.

"I think they would be taller than humans," Henry said. "And they'd live in forests and be really good with bows and arrows."

"And they would be very beautiful," Jessie added.

Dr. Iris chuckled. "So even among the four of you, we have some very different ideas of elves. It shows us that one word can mean many things. We shouldn't think our definition is the only one. Now what about trolls? Our next stop is in the mountains, where there are stories of them too."

"Trolls live under bridges and eat goats," Benny said. "Jessie read me a story where that happened. The troll in the pictures was mean looking."

"I think they would be bigger than the one in that story," Violet said. "I've heard they are so big they can make the ground shake."

"Some people think of trolls as cute, little things,"

Jessie said. "Like those little dolls you can buy."

"In some stories, they aren't very smart," Henry added. "And they'll turn to stone if sunlight hits them."

"So just like with elves, people think about trolls in all different ways," Dr. Iris said. "That is something important to consider for our program." She slowed the car down and pulled over to the side of the road.

"Why are we stopping? There's nothing here," Todd said.

Dr. Iris pointed out the window. "Look over there. What do you see?"

"I don't see anything," Benny said. "It's too foggy."

"I see a little building, I think," Violet said. "But there's grass growing on the roof!"

"You're right," Dr. Iris said. "The building is called a turf house, and it's very old. For a long time, that was the main kind of house people built in Iceland. Let's go take a closer look."

They got out of the car and Todd took out his camera equipment. "I want to film you walking up to

44

the house and looking at it and then walking around it," he said.

As they walked toward the house, the fog got thicker. Violet looked back at the car. It seemed far away. Ahead of them, she could see the building wasn't in good shape. There was no door, just a dark opening where a door might have been.

When they reached the house, Benny pointed to a small sign next to it. "I can read the 'No entrance.' What does the rest of it say?"

"'Restoration underway,'" Violet read out loud.

"That's too bad," Dr. Iris said. "I thought it might be open for us to go inside. I read they are turning this one into a museum, but it appears they aren't done yet. There are very few of these older houses left. At least we can look around the outside."

"Why doesn't it have any windows?" Violet asked peering inside. "It's so dark in there."

"Glass for windows was not available for the first settlers. Later on, when they could get it, it would have been very expensive," Dr. Iris explained. "And any other kind of window covering would have let in cold air, so they decided it was better to have warmth than light."

They walked all around the building. "See how they built it?" Dr. Iris pointed at the roof. "Remember Elin said the early settlers of Iceland didn't realize that trees were so hard to grow here? There were lots of stones and soil though. The builders stacked rows of stones on the bottom to keep the moisture down, and then they cut sections of the ground and stacked them like blocks. The little wood they could get was used on the inside, to make supports for the roof, which was also made of turf. Since the grass on it gets rain and sun, it continues to grow."

"They were very resourceful," said Henry. "They used what they had."

"Kind of like how we did when we lived in the boxcar," said Jessie.

"We should build a house like this in our backyard!" Benny said. "It doesn't look that hard."

Dr. Iris laughed. "I don't know how happy James

would be if you cut up the lawn. But you are right: these turf houses are a reminder that Icelanders have always worked with what they have and made the best of it."

"Move that way," Todd called, pointing to one side. "I want to get some footage of just the house now."

Dr. Iris rubbed her hands together. It was a chilly morning, and the fog seemed to get thicker. "Let's head back to the car and warm up."

They had only gone a few feet before Violet stopped. "Did you see that?" She took a few steps closer to Jessie.

"What?" Jessie asked. "I don't see anything."

"There was something in the fog," Violet said.

"Did it look like an elf?" Benny asked. He ran forward but stopped before he got too far away. "Do you still see it?"

"No," Violet said. "But there was something moving a second ago. It looked like a flash of gray."

"If it wasn't an elf, what could it be?" Benny's voice was shaky.

"I'm sure it was just the fog," Henry said. "If you

watch it, you can kind of see it swirling around."

"Wait. Stop," Jessie said. "Do you feel that?"

Henry shook his head.

"It felt like another earthquake," Jessie said. "But smaller this time."

Benny ran back to the others. His eyes were big. "What if it's giant trolls, like the ones Violet talked about?"

"It could have been another earthquake," Dr. Iris said. "In places where they are common, there can actually be hundreds of small earthquakes in a day. Most are so small people don't notice them."

Violet crossed her arms and shivered. "Why does Iceland have so many earthquakes and volcanoes?"

"Those are good questions," said Dr. Iris. "Let's go warm up in the car and talk about that. Todd, are you finished?"

"Yes," Todd said. "I got some fantastic shots. Love the fog. Whoops!"

"What's wrong?" Violet called. They could barely see him.

"Nothing," Todd answered. "Just tripped over my shoelace."

Once inside the car, Dr. Iris turned on the engine. While it warmed up, she turned in her seat to face the children. Todd sat in the passenger seat going over the footage he had taken.

"I have a feeling we are going to find the earthquakes in Iceland are important for our investigation into its creatures," said Dr. Iris. "Benny, you said it felt like the mountain was moving. And in some ways, it was."

"Because of giant, stony trolls?" asked Benny.

Dr. Iris shook her head. "No, but the earth's surface is made up of moving parts." She held out her hands and then brought them together. "The planet's crust is made up of pieces that fit together like a giant puzzle. Except they don't fit together as nicely as puzzle pieces, and sometimes they shift around. This movement causes earthquakes. Iceland just happens to sit right on a place where two plates meet, so there is a lot of activity here. But not from giant trolls."

As they drove, Violet couldn't stop thinking about what she had seen in the fog. She knew that there was a good explanation for the shaking ground, but what she had seen wasn't just fog. There had been something by the turf house.

She had an idea. "Todd, can I see the footage you took from the turf house?"

"Yeah," said Benny. "I want to see how I look on camera!"

Todd scowled, but Dr. Iris motioned for him to give Violet his video camera. "Just be careful with it," he said. "That is a very expensive piece of equipment."

Violet was interested in seeing the turf house. It really was beautiful. But she was looking for something else too. As she played the footage, she saw the Aldens go around the turf house. Then, as the children were walking out of the frame, Violet noticed a flash of gray, just like the one she had seen. She could see what looked like long legs and a body. She tried to pause the footage to get a better view. But just as she did, Dr. Iris slammed on the brakes. Violet's finger slipped and accidentally hit the delete button.

The car skidded to a stop, and the children looked out the front window. Ahead, the road disappeared into a stream.

"There's no bridge!" cried Benny.

"The person at the rental shop mentioned streams like this. With the melting ice, sometimes you just have to drive through them," Dr. Iris explained. She leaned forward to get a better view. "This one looks like it's a few inches."

"Should we turn back?" asked Jessie.

While Henry took out the road map, Violet handed back Todd's camera and explained what had happened.

"I'm so sorry," she said. "It was an accident."

Todd opened his mouth to speak, but Dr. Iris spoke first. "Oh, no need to worry about that, Violet," said Dr. Iris. "Todd will have plenty of time to get footage. Besides, we have bigger things to worry about. Right, Todd?"

Todd scowled.

Henry found where they were on the map. "We'd have to go miles out of our way to find a bridge," he said.

Dr. Iris nodded. "Thank you, Henry." She looked over the stream one last time. "I've driven through deeper than this. Now, hang on, everyone!"

A ROCKY START

Water sprayed to both sides of the car as Dr. Iris steered into the stream. Benny looked out the window. "We're sinking!" he said.

"It's just the water getting deeper," Henry said. "It will be okay."

When they were almost to the other side, a thud came from the front of the car. Dr. Iris stopped accelerating. The car tipped a little to one side.

"I don't like this," Todd said. "I don't want water

coming in and getting my cameras wet."

"The way the car is tipping, I think we have a flat tire," Henry said.

"Yes, we'll have to get it back up on the road to change it." Dr. Iris pushed down on the gas pedal, but they did not move.

"We're stuck!" Violet cried.

"We're spinning our wheels," said Henry. "Let's get out and push. It's shallow enough."

Dr. Iris turned around. She still had a smile on her face. "Yes, good idea. It's all part of going on an adventure: expect the unexpected."

"This wasn't part of my job description," Todd grumbled as he opened his door. He let out a little shriek when he stepped in the water. "It's cold!"

As Henry, Jessie, and Todd went to the back of the car to help push, Violet and Benny turned to the back of the car to cheer them on. As they did, something caught Violet's eye. Everyone's luggage had moved around a little, and the flap to Todd's camera bag was open. Inside, she could see a large stone. So *that* was what he had picked up at the gas station the day before.

With Henry, Jessie, and Todd pushing, and Benny cheering loudly, they made it far enough across the stream that Dr. Iris could drive up onto the road. It didn't take long to change the tire.

"Why doesn't everyone put on dry shoes and socks, and then we might as well eat lunch?" said Dr. Iris. "I've got a basket in the back with our food in it."

Todd changed out of his wet clothes first, and when he was done, Violet noticed that he buckled up the flap on his camera bag. Why had he taken a rock?

After Henry and Jessie had changed, Jessie got out the basket and passed around sandwiches.

"I think we all should have an extra sandwich from all this hard work," said Benny.

"Benny, you stayed in the car while we pushed," Henry said.

"Cheering is hard work too!" he said.

"We only have enough for one each," said Jessie.

But when Benny unwrapped his sandwich, a funny smell rose from it.

He wrinkled his nose. "I don't think I like this kind of Icelandic food."

Dr. Iris smelled the sandwich. "It smells like it's spoiled, Benny."

"Mine is spoiled too," Jessie said. "How did it go bad? The expiration date is for next month."

"Remember, Iceland has to import a lot of their food," Dr. Iris said. "Sometimes it may not be shipped or stored right along the way."

Todd sighed. "Mine is bad too."

"Mine is okay," Violet said. "And Henry's too. We'll share." She broke the sandwiches into pieces.

"At least the chocolate won't have gone bad," Dr. Iris said.

"Chocolate?" Benny said. "You guys can have my sandwich!"

Dr. Iris laughed. "Your grandfather might forgive me for driving across that stream. But I don't think he'd be too happy if I let you eat only chocolate." After everyone had finished the sandwiches, she handed out chocolate bars.

"We certainly aren't having much luck," said Todd. "First that earthquake knocked me off of a rock. And now we got a flat tire. It's almost like we're cursed."

"These things happen when you're traveling. Just minor problems," Dr. Iris said. "Let's get back on our way."

They'd driven several more miles when Todd said, "I'd like to get some more footage for the show." He motioned to the right. "That landscape looks great. Can we get a little closer?"

Dr. Iris turned and drove down a rough road that ended right in front of a big rock formation. As she slowed down, the engine sputtered and then quit.

"Uh-oh," Violet said.

"Now what?" Todd asked.

"It sounds like the car has run out of gas," Henry said.

"You're right, but I don't understand it." Dr. Iris tapped at the gas gauge. "I filled it full at the station yesterday. We haven't driven far."

Henry got out of the car and walked around to the back. "It smell like gas," he said. "We must have damaged something when we crossed the stream."

Todd got out too. "Someone will come along. I'm sure by the time I'm done filming, someone will be here to help us."

Dr. Iris picked up her cell phone. "I can't get a signal."

"Henry and I can go out to the turnoff and flag down someone who will help us," Jessie suggested.

Dr. Iris nodded. "As soon as Todd is finished, I'll send him to join you. If someone comes along and stops before he gets there, ask if they will give Todd a lift to the nearest service station. I'm afraid we are going to need a tow truck if there really is a leak in a gas line."

Jessie and Henry waited for about a half hour and didn't see a single vehicle. Todd joined them but didn't say much. He was too busy looking at the footage he had taken.

"I see a car!" Henry said at last. Henry and Jessie

waved until the car slowed down and stopped.

A man rolled down his window. "Something wrong?" he asked.

Jessie explained what had happened.

"That does sound like a leak in a gas line," the man said. "There's a service station about twenty miles from here. I can give one of you a lift there if you'd like to arrange a tow."

Todd sighed. "I'll go. What a trip this is turning out to be, and it's only the second day."

He climbed in. When the car drove off, Jessie and Henry went back to wait with the others.

"I'm going to walk around a little and see if I can get a better cell phone signal," Dr. Iris said. "I want the guesthouse owner to know we are going to be late."

When Dr. Iris walked away, Violet turned around and leaned over the back seat, staring into the cargo area. She'd had a lot of time to think while everyone was gone.

"I know why everything is going wrong," she

told Henry and Jessie and Benny. She explained about how Todd had picked up a lava rock and put it in his bag.

"So you think all of this is because of that rock?" said Henry. "How?"

"I get it," Benny said. "It might be an elf rock! Like those stories about how the workers moved the rock and everything went bad."

Jessie looked unsure. "We've had bad luck. But there are other possible explanations. Like Dr. Iris said, unexcepted things happen on trips."

"And all the other things haven't been that bad," said Henry. "The dent in the car and the goose chasing Todd were Todd's own fault."

"I didn't know about the dent!" said Violet. "What happened?"

Henry told the others about what had happened that morning at the Graylag Goose.

"Okay," said Benny. "That's a lot of bad stuff happening. Maybe we really are cursed!"

"It can't be an elf rock," Henry said. "If it's in a

bag back there, it can't be that big."

"Remember," Violet said, "Dr. Iris said people believe the elves can do magic and make the space inside the rocks bigger."

Benny said, "I want to look at this rock."

Henry opened his door and everyone followed him to the back of the car. "Let me move Todd's cameras. If he complains, I can tell him I did it."

Henry shifted bags around so they could pick up the rock.

Benny held it up to his ear and listened, just as he had done at the elf rock. "I wish the elves would come out and talk to us if they are in there." He set it down and tapped on the rock. "Hello!"

Jessie took a closer look. The rock was big and bulky. "It's a volcano rock, like the elf rock we saw. But otherwise it just looks normal."

Henry shook his head. He felt a little silly looking at a rock so closely. "Let's put it back before Todd or Dr. Iris comes back."

After a little while, Dr. Iris returned. "I got a

signal and spoke to the guesthouse owner and to Todd. He'll be back soon."

The tow truck didn't take long to arrive, and a car followed behind.

A man got out of the tow truck. "When we heard you were out here with children, my wife decided to come along and give you a ride while I tow the car."

Benny was still worried from talking about Todd's rock. "We got stuck in a river and then our tire exploded and our food went bad," he said. "We think we might be cursed!"

The tow truck driver gave Benny a friendly smile. "In Iceland we have a saying: *þetta reddast*."

"What does that mean?" Violet asked.

"'It will all work out in the end,'" the man said. "When you live on an island shaped by volcanoes, unexpected things happen. You can't worry about the small things."

The man taught them to say the word. "Thet-ta red-ust," Benny repeated. "It will all work out in the end." Saying the words made him feel better.

"Where are you heading?" the woman asked, and Dr. Iris told her the name of the guesthouse.

"Oh, I know Gunnar, the man who owns it!" the woman said. "When we get to the repair shop, you can get your bags out of your car, and I'll take you there. It's not far at all."

"Well, that is a welcome coincidence!" said Dr. Iris. "Thank you."

"You were right!" Benny told the tow truck driver. "It really did work out okay!"

CHAPTER 6

STORIES IN THE DARK

By the time they got to the guesthouse, the children were feeling back to normal. But Benny's stomach was rumbling. "Will we be able to eat soon?" he asked.

"I have a feeling that will work out too." Dr. Iris winked. "But first I have a surprise for you. Your grandfather said you liked surprises."

The Aldens thanked the woman for the ride, and Dr. Iris led them around the side of the guesthouse, where there was a field of grazing horses.

"Do those horses belong to the guesthouse?" Violet asked. "Will we get to ride them?"

Dr. Iris nodded. "We are going on a horseback trek the day after tomorrow. We'll be going to an abandoned town on the coast."

"Awesome!" Henry said.

"I can't wait!" Jessie added. She had read all about Icelandic horses and couldn't wait to ride one.

Just then, a tall man with a broad face and a big smile came out of the guesthouse. "Welcome!" He introduced himself and told the children to call him Gunnar. "Let's get your bags inside."

Violet wasn't happy to see the rock in Todd's bag go inside with them. While things were looking up on their trip, she hoped nothing else would go wrong.

"You must be hungry after your adventures today," Gunnar said. "I can take you over to the café if you are ready to eat."

"I am very ready to eat!" said Benny.

The children put their suitcases in their room, which was similar to the one they had stayed in at

Elin's, except instead of being decorated with wooden birds, there were photographs of the horses.

A sign above the café read *The Elf Café*.

"Is it owned by elves?" Benny asked.

"It's just the name," Dr. Iris said. "We're near a famous elf rock that people come to visit."

"It would be really fun to go to a café owned by elves," Jessie said. "Though I don't know what kind of food they would serve."

"It would be invisible!" Benny said. "I don't think invisible food would taste good."

Gunnar let out a loud laugh. "You're right. And it would be hard to eat!"

They went inside, and a waitress came to their table. "The soup and bread are always very good," she said as she handed them menus.

"Yes, we eat quite a bit of soup in Iceland. It keeps us warm on chilly days," Gunnar said.

Dr. Iris rubbed her hands together. "I'm chilly now, so soup sounds just right."

It had been a long day, but they felt better eating

a warm meal. While they ate, Gunnar asked what the children had seen so far on their trip. Benny told him about the elf rock at Elin's.

"She said that people in Iceland don't want elf rocks moved," Violet added. She looked at Todd. "The elves could get angry."

"Some people do believe that, especially some older people," Gunnar replied. "I like to think of it a different way. We value our heritage, and if stories passed on from one generation to the next tell us that invisible beings live in a certain place, we respect that and consider those rocks cultural treasure."

"Have you ever seen an elf?" Violet asked.

"No, but you are going to meet my mother after dinner. She can tell you what she knows about elves and about trolls. She grew up close to here on a farm. Back then, their house was the only one for miles around. She used to tell me stories about how her grandmother said she'd played with the elves when she was a little girl because there were no other children around."

"Is that true?" Henry asked.

"That's the story her grandmother told," Gunnar said. "Who can say if it is true or not? Listen and see what you think. Now, if everyone is finished with their dinner, we can go back to the guesthouse and hear some stories."

Gunnar took them to a big room at the back of the guesthouse that was full of sofas and chairs. An old woman sat by the fireplace. The room was nice and warm. She smiled at them when they came in.

"This is my mother, Helga Olafsdottir," Gunnar introduced the children, and everyone sat down.

The old woman nodded. "Welcome. I'm so glad to hear you want to know some of our stories."

"What's that noise?" Violet asked. "It sounds like drumming." She held very still in case it was another earthquake.

"Just the rain," Helga said. "We have a tin roof on the building, so when the rain hits it, it sounds very loud. Rainy nights are good nights for stories. Now, I know you have heard about elves, but up here near the mountains, we also talk about trolls, especially around Christmastime. Would you like to hear one of those stories?"

The children nodded.

"Our most famous troll may be one named Grýla. Some people say she is part troll and part ogre. Do you know what an ogre is?" she asked Benny. He shook his head.

"An ogre is like a monster, but it looks a little bit like a human. Grýla has a big nose and enormous hands with long fingers." The old woman reached out her hands and made grabbing motions.

Benny was so startled that he leaped backward in his chair.

"Oh, much bigger hands than mine, Benny," Helga said, chuckling. "I didn't mean to frighten you. Don't worry. I'm not fierce like Grýla. She lives in the mountains with her husband and her thirteen sons. They are not nice at all. They steal farmers' sheep and cows. And right before Christmas, it is said that Grýla and her sons come down from the mountains so Grýla can catch naughty children."

The woman paused, and Benny and Violet looked at each other.

"What...what does she do with them?" Violet asked, though she wasn't sure she wanted to know.

"She'd like to boil them in her cauldron." Helga made a stirring motion with her hand. "But she can only capture children who misbehave, and if they say they are sorry, she must release them. Not only is Grýla prowling about, but her sons are also out, ready to make mischief. We call them the Yule Lads. Icelandic children place a shoe in their bedroom window each evening on the thirteen days before Christmas. Every night, one Yule Lad visits. They leave sweets and small gifts for good children, but bad children get rotting potatoes!" Helga pinched her nose. "Those potatoes smell very bad!"

The lights flickered, and one of the windows rattled. "What's happening?" Benny said. He grabbed onto the sides of his chair.

"Just the storm picking up." Gunnar went over to

check the latch on the window. They could hear the wind whistling outside.

"I'm not sure I like trolls," Benny said. "Can we hear stories about elves? One that isn't scary?"

"Of course." Helga's calm voice was comforting with the sounds coming from outside. "Most elf stories are happy stories."

She looked up at a picture sitting on the fireplace mantel. "The boy in that picture is my brother. He had a strange thing happen to him one time. He had the job of taking the sheep up to the mountain pastures in the summer, and he had to stay with them for weeks by himself. One night, there was a bad storm. The sheep got frightened and scattered. My brother tried hard to find them all the next day, and he rounded up most of them, but he knew a few were missing. All of a sudden, a boy appeared—a boy my brother had never seen before. The boy offered to help him find the sheep. By the end of the day, they got them all back together, but when my brother went to thank the boy, he was gone. My brother never saw him again."

"Was the boy an elf?" Violet asked.

"I don't know, but my brother thought he might have been. My mother thought that one time she saw elves, too, special elves, the king and queen of the elves in East Iceland."

"Wow!" Benny said. "I didn't know elves had kings and queens."

"Elves in Iceland do. My mother had been out collecting wild herbs, and she sat down for a while to rest. The sun was warm, and she had gotten up very early that morning, so she fell asleep. When she woke up, she was amazed to see a group of people riding by. A regal-looking man and woman rode in front. They all wore fine, beautiful clothes in all different colors, clothes like she'd never seen before. She only had the clothes her mother wove for her from sheep wool, and none of it was in the pretty colors she loved. People were very poor in those days."

"What happened next?" Jessie asked.

"They rode behind the rock, and my mother wanted so badly to see more of them that she ran after them. But once she went around the rock herself, she didn't see anything. They were gone. She never forgot that day. She was sure she had seen the elf queen and king, and she said when she grew up, if she had the money, she would buy herself a red skirt just like the elf queen wore."

"Did she get to buy a red skirt?" Violet asked.

The old woman smiled. "She certainly did, and she bought me one too. She loved those skirts."

Violet liked hearing these stories of elves. They sounded so much more peaceful.

Suddenly, the lights began to flicker. Then they went dark.

"Oh, great," Todd said.

"We don't often lose power in the summer," said Gunnar. "This storm is unusually strong. Stay here. I've got some lanterns we can use." He brought out lanterns with lights inside that looked like candles.

"The candles remind me of the old days," Gunnar's mother said. "If you come again in the winter, you'll see many candles in the windows of people's homes.

It was believed that on New Year's Eve, the hidden people moved to new locations, so some Icelanders left candles in their houses to help the elves find their way. When I was a little girl, I liked to look out the window to look for elves in the night. It felt good to know we were helping them, because usually they didn't need any help."

For a little while, everyone sat in silence, thinking about the nice story. Then Todd gave a very loud sneeze. "I'm getting a cold," he said. "I don't understand it. I never get sick."

"I think it is a good time for all of us to go to bed," Dr. Iris said.

"Thank you for the stories," Jessie said to Helga. "We won't forget them."

"Good," Helga said. "Stories need to be remembered."

Back in their room, the Aldens got ready to go to sleep.

"I liked the story about the elf queen and king and the red skirt," Jessie said as she climbed into bed.

"Do you think the story is true?" Violet asked.

"The mother might have dreamed it," said Henry. "She could have been sleeping and thought she'd woken up. That happens in dreams sometimes."

"Well, I hope I don't wake up at all tonight," said Benny, letting out a big yawn. "Not even in my dreams."

Soon the children blew out their candles and laid down to sleep. But Violet's mind was still thinking. Helga's elf stories had been so nice. She liked the idea of elves and humans helping each other. She wanted to believe that the hidden elves were friendly. But if bad things kept happening, she wasn't sure if she could.

CHAPTER 7

FACES IN THE STONE

The next morning when Violet woke up, she was happy to see the electricity had come back on and to hear that nothing bad had happened in the night.

At breakfast, Dr. Iris said, "Those were wonderful stories Helga told us last night, don't you think?" The waitress had brought them cinnamon rolls and a special kind of Icelandic yogurt called *skyr*. They were all so busy eating, no one replied to Dr. Iris right away.

Jessie spoke up first. "I'm glad we saw the turf house and how much empty space there is in Iceland before we heard them," she said. "It makes it easier to imagine how it would be to live out where you don't see other people very often. It would make it easier to believe there were elves to keep you company."

"The stories about trolls were scary," Benny said. "I don't know why people want to tell stories about scary things."

"That's an interesting observation, Benny," Dr. Iris said. "Why would people tell stories about frightening things?"

"Sometimes scary stories are fun when you know they aren't real," Jessie said. "Like ghost stories."

"We learned in school that, a long time ago, people made up stories to explain things they didn't understand," Henry said. "I remember a story about Greek gods and that people thought lightning came from the gods fighting, throwing bolts of fire at each other."

"Yes, those are both good reasons. We'll keep those in mind while we find out more. Today's trip is to a place I've wanted to see for a long time. When the lava from a volcanic eruption fell over a lake, it hardened into all kinds of shapes. People think it looks like the remains of an ancient city. They even named it *Dimmuborgir*, which means 'dark castle.'"

"Do people think there are elves there too?" Violet said.

"No, but some people think trolls have lived there or visit the site at certain times of the year."

"I hope they aren't there now," said Benny.

"How are we going to get there?" Henry asked. "Is the car fixed?"

"No, I rented another from town," Dr. Iris said. "It has already been delivered."

By the time they were finished, the rain had gotten worse, and Todd was very grumpy when he got in the car. He sneezed. "Will we be able to see anything with all this rain?" he asked.

"It's supposed to clear up," Dr. Iris said. "Remember what we learned yesterday? It will all work out in the end."

Dr. Iris was right. By the time she parked the car, the rain had stopped.

Henry looked out the window. Ahead, lava rocks rose up like two towers, and a pathway ran between them. It almost looked like they were on another planet.

"This is fantastic!" Todd said, suddenly cheering up. He jumped out of the car and went around to the cargo area to get out his camera. "The gray clouds are great for this. It adds to the atmosphere. Now, if it doesn't rain anymore, I can get some great shots."

"Don't climb on any of the formations," Dr. Iris said to Todd as he grabbed his camera bag and headed off. "The lava is fragile and might collapse. And stay out of the roped-off areas! They protect birds' nests and vegetation."

Todd was already down the path.

"I'm not sure he was listening," Dr. Iris said.

"He does get really focused on filming," Jessie said.

"All right, this is a big area," Dr. Iris said. "According-ing to the guidebook, it's easy to get lost if you get off a path. Some of the formations look so much alike, people can't remember if they've seen them before, so they don't know if they are going in circles or not. Just remember that as you are exploring. I need to make a phone call. We'll meet back here in an hour."

"I wonder if she's checking on the volcano," Henry said as they headed down one of the paths.

"Probably," Jessie said. "She was talking to Gunnar about it this morning before we went to breakfast."

"Look over there!" Violet cried. "That looks like a big castle wall. And the hole in the middle is where there would have been a gate."

"That looks like a face, like a big troll with his mouth open," said Benny.

"Benny, that's just because you have trolls on the mind," said Jessie. But even Jessie had to admit that some of the stones did look like faces.

"Some stories do say that trolls will turn to stone

if they are caught in sunlight," Henry said. "I can see why people believe that with all these rocks that look like troll faces."

As they followed the path, Jessie tried to keep track of the turns, but after a little while, the fog came back, making it hard to get a sense of direction. The wind picked up, so the fog swirled around them.

"The fog makes it extra eerie," Henry said.

"But it makes it easier to imagine we are walking through an ancient city," Jessie said.

Violet pointed ahead. "This looks like it could have been a row of shops," she said. "And that looks like a dragon's head, like it's lying down on the ground. And the hole on that part would be its eye."

Benny drew close to Jessie. "It's so quiet."

"The fog is muffling sound." Jessie checked her watch. "We should go back. We've come a long ways, and it will be time to meet Dr. Iris soon."

"I hope we can find our way," said Benny as they started down the path.

"I do too," said Jessie. She seemed unsure.

Suddenly, there was a noise behind them. When the children turned around, they saw something moving through the fog.

Benny grabbed Jessie's hand. "It's a troll!"

Two narrow legs appeared. "It's like the shape I saw at the turf house!" said Violet.

As the shape got closer, the children could see that it was taller than they were. It's head popped through the fog.

"A horse!" said Jessie.

The animal blew air out of its nose. It seemed happy to see them.

"It must have gotten loose during the storm last night," said Henry. "Let's head back and let Dr. Iris know we saw it."

The children followed the horse as it went back up the trail.

"It's almost like it knows the way back," said Benny.

As the fog got thicker, they lost sight of the horse. When they emerged, they were at the parking lot with Dr. Iris.

"Where did the horse go?" asked Violet.

"Horse?" said Dr. Iris.

"We were following a horse down the trail," said Jessie. "Didn't you see it?"

"I didn't see anything come by the car," Dr. Iris said. "But maybe I missed it. I've been trying to get ahold of Todd."

"It reminds me of the story of Helga's mother," said Jessie. "She looked around the rock and they were gone."

"It really did sneak off." Henry scratched his head. "Oh well, I'm just glad it helped us find our way out."

"Well, I hope a horse—real or not—finds Todd and brings him out," said Dr. Iris.

They called Todd's name, but he didn't answer.

Dr. Iris sighed. "We'll never find him in all this fog. We'll just have to wait until it clears. Then we can go look for him."

"I knew more bad things would happen," Violet said, wringing her hands.

"I'm sure he's just taking pictures," Jessie said.

They called again, but Todd didn't answer. Just as they were heading back to the car to warm up, Todd emerged from the fog.

"Didn't you hear us calling?" Dr. Iris asked.

"No, I was concentrating on getting the angle for the shot just right. This place is amazing!"

"I'm glad the trolls didn't get you," Benny told him.

"Thanks, kid," Todd said as he got in the car. "But I'd let myself be captured if I could get a photo of that. It would be history-making!"

As Dr. Iris drove out of the parking lot, she asked, "What did you think of the place?"

"I can see why people have stories about trolls here," Henry said. "Especially if you came here from a country that didn't look the same. It would be a way to make sense of why the rocks looked so different."

"That's a good point, Henry," Dr. Iris said. "Tomorrow we'll see a different type of landscape when we ride to the coast. We'll see if that helps us understand the legends we've been investigating."

"It will be fun to investigate by riding horses," Jessie said.

"Yes, it certainly will," Dr. Iris replied. "An investigation and an adventure."

CHAPTER 8

RIDE TO THE COAST

When Dr. Iris pulled into the parking lot of the guesthouse, Gunnar was outside doing yardwork. He waved at them as they got out of the car. Benny looked toward the field. "Can I go down to the fence to see the horses?"

"We can all go. I'll introduce you to the ones you are riding tomorrow," Gunnar said. They followed him down, and he whistled as they walked. Several of the horses trotted over to the fence at the sound.

They were all different colors, but every horse had a long mane and a long tail.

"We saw a horse at Dimmuborgir," Jessie said. "We thought one might have gotten out in the storm."

Gunnar shook his head. "All of my horses are here. It's possible someone else is missing one, but I am the closest horse owner to that area."

The children pet the horses for a little while. One of them licked at Benny's hand, thinking he was going to get fed.

"Horses here look more like ponies," Henry said. "They're smaller. And…um…wider."

Gunnar reached over the fence and patted a reddish-brown one. "Icelandic horses are smaller than other horses, but they are very hardy. The first ones were brought by the Vikings a thousand years ago. Over the years, they adapted to the climate and the limited amount of foliage."

"So not only people, but animals had to adapt too," Dr. Iris said.

"Yes," Gunnar replied. "One way these horses

adapted over many generations is that they have stronger bones than other kinds of horses. That means that even though they look small, they can carry adults—even me! That brown one over there is mine. His name is Hafli. It means 'giant.'"

"Benny, this chestnut one is your horse. His name is Kisi."

"Kissy? Like kissing?" Benny asked. "That's a funny name for a horse."

"No, it's spelled different. K-I-S-I. It means 'cat.' We named him that because he's liked cats since he was a foal. He has a special cat friend who sleeps in the stables."

"Which one is mine?" Violet asked.

"The black-and-white one right in front of you. That's Lappi. See the white bands on her legs? *Lappi* is a word for horses who look like they are wearing socks."

Lappi reached her head over the fence and nuzzled Violet's hair. "Hey, that tickles!" Violet said.

"I think she likes you," Gunnar said.

"I like her too!"

"Jessie, you get Elfur, the gray one with the white markings and the white mane. You can probably guess what Elfur means."

"Elf?"

"Yes! She is such a beautiful color, we couldn't think of a better name."

Gunnar moved over to a white horse. "Henry, this one is yours. Meet Nennir; it means 'ghost.' He's a little jumpy, but when Dr. Perez made the arrangements for the trip, she said she'd been told you were a good rider."

Henry nodded and walked over to pet the horse.

Todd's horse was a speckled one named Depla, and Dr. Iris got one named Vindur, a horse with a silver mane.

After meeting the horses, Gunnar took them to a small storage room off the front door and showed them their saddlebags. "Pack what you need for a few days. We have some supplies and sleeping bags stored in an old house near our campsite, so we don't need to carry everything."

The next morning, Violet was so excited she could hardly eat breakfast, even though the waitress had brought them a big platter of waffles and bowls of berries. They were almost finished when Dr. Iris came in to the café. She had a worried look on her face.

"Is there news about the volcano?" Henry asked.

"A little. The eruption is still happening, but at this point the ash and smoke are being blown to the south, opposite of where we are. Gunnar is bringing a radio set, so we can monitor it. We'll keep our fingers crossed."

The horses seemed eager to go. The group headed north and rode out into the open spaces until the guesthouse and the café were out of sight. They saw no one except for some sheep who stared at them as they passed by.

"It feels like we could be part of a fairy tale," Violet said. Even though she knew Todd had the rock in his bag, she didn't feel so worried riding Lappi.

"Yes, especially because there is no one else out here," Jessie said. "Iceland is like an enchanted land."

"If some little girl is asleep in a field and she wakes up, maybe she'll think we are elves," Benny said. He looked down at his jacket. "Except we don't have on fancy elf clothes."

"It's like a fantasy story, where people go on a quest," Henry said.

"We are on a quest in a way," Dr. Iris said. "A quest for information. We've heard the stories. Now we are going to a village where many people have reported elf sightings over the years."

Henry pointed in front of them. "I see a stream ahead."

"Do we go right through it?" Jessie asked Gunnar.

"Yes, the horses like to splash through the water," he replied. Violet's horse sped up. "Especially Lappi!" Gunnar called as Violet and Lappi went through first.

"At least a horse can't have a flat tire!" Benny said as he and Kisi followed Violet. Henry's horse, Nennir, acted like he didn't want to cross, but Henry urged him on until he went through.

Henry rode his horse up next to Gunnar's. "How do

people figure out where they are going?" Henry asked. "It's so empty out here, and there aren't any landmarks."

"Good question. I know the way because I've been this route so many times, but I also carry a GPS in my saddlebag, just in case. It is too easy to get lost."

As they rode on, a rumbling sound came from the distance. "Oh, the trolls must be angry with each other," Gunnar said.

"Really?" Benny asked.

"He is teasing, Benny," said Henry. "It's just thunder."

Gunnar laughed. "I am teasing. I like to tease. If you listen closely, you should hear something else soon. We're getting very close to a waterfall and the ocean."

They rode up over a ridge to see the ocean below them.

"Beautiful," Dr. Iris said.

"Look that way and you'll see something even more spectacular." Gunnar pointed to the left.

The ridge met a steep cliff where a waterfall

poured down into a stream. The stream ran all the way down into the ocean.

"We'll ride down so you can get a better look," said Gunnar.

As they drew closer, they could see a big building right on the shore. It had once been white, but some of the paint had worn off, leaving gray blotches. The windows were all covered over with large sheets of metal.

Beyond the building, some small houses were scattered around a big, flat area. They looked rundown, like no one lived in them. Some of their windows were boarded up too.

"There isn't anyone living here, is there?" Jessie asked.

"No, the village was abandoned years ago. It was built for the people who worked at that building, the big one on the shore. That was a fish cannery, and fishermen brought in the herring catch to be packed into cans. The area got overfished though. They caught so many, there weren't enough left for the next season. We know now much more about how to manage natural resources like fish, but they didn't back then, and the cannery had to close."

"It's kind of spooky with all the empty buildings," Violet said.

Todd got off his horse and took a camera out of his saddlebag. "Empty buildings are wonderful to photograph. What's inside the cannery?" he asked.

"Some of the old equipment, but it's too dangerous to go in," Gunnar said. "I don't know the condition of the floors, and what equipment is left is surely rusted. You wouldn't want to hurt yourself on any of that. And there isn't any electricity in there these days, so it's dark with the windows covered up."

"Too bad. Some of my best shots have been of old factories." Todd moved off and began to photograph the cannery from different angles.

Gunnar moved to get off of Hafli, but when he put his foot on the ground, he cried out in pain and fell down to one side.

Henry moved quickly to try to help him up, but

Gunnar said, "Wait. I've hurt my ankle."

"I saw your foot twist when you put it down," Dr. Iris said.

Gunnar sighed. "Yes, I should have been paying more attention. This is my bad ankle. I sprained it a few years ago, and it's been weak ever since."

"You should prop it up if it's a sprain," Jessie said. "I learned that in a first-aid class."

"Yes, we should get you to the campsite," Dr. Iris said. "The faster you get it elevated, the better."

It took both Henry and Todd to help Gunnar up. He tried to put weight on his foot but grimaced when he did. "I'm afraid you're going to have to give me a boost so I can get back on Hafli," he said.

"I knew something else would go wrong," Violet said to Benny as they watched Todd and Henry help Gunnar.

Benny nodded. "I really wish Todd hadn't brought that rock along."

Todd started to walk back to the cannery. "I'll stay here for a while longer. I want to take more photos."

"Gunnar is going to need your help at the campsite," Dr. Iris said.

"Sorry," Gunnar added. "But you can come back tomorrow. The campsite is at the house on the far side of the village." He looked up at the sky, which had clouded over. "In fact, I think we'll stay in the house instead of camping tonight. It's going to rain."

Gunnar acted cheerful on the ride to the campsite, but when they got there, he couldn't put any weight on his ankle at all. The house next to the campsite looked like someone was trying to fix it up. It had a new porch that hadn't yet been painted. There was a building nearby that was just a roof over some poles.

"We bought this property for our treks," Gunnar said. "It's nice to have a building to store some supplies in and to give shelter if the weather gets too bad. Most tourists don't like to camp in tents when it's raining." He pointed to the other building. "That's for the horses. The roof provides some cover for them. We tie them up so they don't decide to go exploring."

The old house had two stories. There was a kitchen at the back and two smaller rooms in the front. "The bedrooms are upstairs," Gunnar said. "The saddle stands are in one of the front rooms on this floor. We don't know what the room was used for originally, but we call it the dining room, because we also keep oats for the horses in there."

The oats were in a big metal bin. Gunnar told them how much to feed the horses. "Make sure you seal it up tight when you are done. Mice would be happy to get in there and have a feast."

The Aldens finished taking care of the horses just as it started to rain. Then Jessie and Henry helped Dr. Iris cook dinner after Gunnar explained what supplies they had stored away. After they had eaten, Dr. Iris yawned. "I don't know about the rest of you, but I'm tired. Why don't we clean up and then go to sleep? It's been a long day."

"Remember, nobody wander off tonight. Trolls might capture you!" Gunnar said. Then he laughed. "Benny, you should see the look on your face. I like to tease, remember. It's something parents in Iceland say to their children. Just imagine how dangerous it would be for children to go off on their own with so few people around. It was a clever way to get children to stay close to home."

"Okay," Benny said. "But I wasn't going to wander off anyway."

"I know. I'm sorry. I shouldn't have teased you."

The Aldens and Dr. Iris took one room upstairs, and Todd took the other. Gunnar stayed on the first floor because his ankle hurt too much to climb the stairs.

The wind blew so hard during the night, Violet kept waking up. Very early in the morning, she was sure she heard footsteps in the hallway. Then she fell back asleep until Benny woke her up. It was still raining, now even harder than the night before.

"We can make breakfast," Jessie said to Gunnar when they all went downstairs. "Just tell us what to make."

"Oatmeal is on the menu," he said. "There is

some in the cabinet along with some dried fruit and nuts."

Henry got out bowls and silverware to set the table.

"Where is Todd?" Dr. Iris asked.

"I thought he was still sleeping," Gunnar said.

"I'll go wake him up," said Henry. He came back a moment later. "He's not there!"

"Maybe he is out taking pictures," Jessie said.

"In this rain?" Dr. Iris stared out the window. "I suppose that's possible. Let's wait a bit and see if he comes back."

After breakfast, Gunnar said it was time to feed the horses.

"You and Dr. Iris can stay here. We can feed them," Henry told Gunnar. "Just tell us how much."

Violet went ahead and got to the horse shelter first. She was happy to see Lappi waiting for her. But something seemed wrong. She counted the horses. There were only six.

"Depla is missing!" she said as the others came in. "Todd must have taken her!"

CHAPTER 9

A DARING RESCUE

Why would Todd go riding in the rain?" Benny asked.

"To take photos somewhere," Henry said. "That seems to be all he thinks about."

"We should check the saddles to see if Depla's is gone," Jessie suggested. "She might have gotten loose. Did anyone look in the dining room this morning?"

No one had.

"I'll go count them," Benny said. He ran back to the house, where he counted only six saddles in the dining room.

He dashed down to the horse shelter. "Depla's saddle is missing too," he reported.

"Todd said he really wanted to photograph the cannery," Violet said. "I think that's where he went. We should go look for him."

Gunnar and Dr. Iris were upset when the children told them where they thought Todd had gone.

"I hope if he went to the cannery he didn't go inside. I told him it was dangerous!" Gunnar said. "If you can't find him, I can radio for help. Someone will come by boat. But there has been some more bad news. The volcano situation is getting worse, and the ashfall has begun to blow this way. We need to get back to the guesthouse as soon as possible."

"How many more things can go wrong?" Violet said.

"We'll find him, and we'll hurry," Henry said.

"We should get flashlights though. I've got one in my backpack."

"Me too," Jessie said.

They retrieved their flashlights and jogged back down to the cannery.

"There's Depla," Violet called as they reached it. The horse was tied to a pole where the building jutted out over the beach. She whinnied when she saw them.

"Todd!" Jessie called out. The others joined in, but there was no response.

"Maybe he can't hear us if he's inside," Violet said.

"I hope he hasn't hurt himself," Dr. Iris said. "He was worried about you children coming along, but he's the one who wanders off."

The big door screeched as Henry pulled it open to reveal a long hallway.

"It's dark in there," Benny said.

Henry shined his flashlight around.

"The place is in better condition inside than it looks on the outside," Dr. Iris said.

Benny shivered. "It's cold and scary though."

Henry tried to open a door off the hallway, but it wouldn't budge. "This door is rusted shut. He couldn't have gone this way." There weren't any other doors on that level.

"We'll have to go up, I suppose," Dr. Iris said, "but we'll go very carefully, one step at a time, to test the stairs and the floor. I'll go first. Wait at the bottom until I'm all the way at the top."

The steps creaked but didn't shake or move.

"They're safe," Dr. Iris called. "But still come up one at a time."

A big door was open off the upstairs hallway. "Todd!" Dr. Iris called into the room.

There was no answer. "Maybe he isn't here," Benny said. "Why would he want to come to such a dark place?"

"He has to be around here somewhere if Depla is outside," Violet said.

They looked into the room, which was a big space full of long tables. A little light shone in where one of the metal sheets had come loose and had sagged down to one side.

"What does the floor look like in there?" Dr. Iris asked. Henry moved the flashlight around. "It looks solid."

"Okay, but go slowly," she said. They went in, their footsteps echoing in the big space.

"Todd!" Jessie called.

"I think I heard something," Violet said. "Over there." She pointed to an opening in the floor.

"What is that ramp thing sticking out?" Benny asked as they made their way over, following Henry's flashlight beam.

"It's a conveyer belt," Henry said. "They must have used it to bring things up from the lower floor."

Violet spotted something on the floor close to the conveyor belt. "Henry, shine your light over here. What is that?"

The light lit up a white blob. "It's Todd's shoe," Henry said.

Jessie tried to see down through the conveyor belt

to the floor below. "It's so dark with all the windows covered up down there."

"Todd?" Dr. Iris called.

"Yes" came a shaky voice. "I'm down here."

"Are you hurt?" Dr. Iris asked.

"I hurt my arm when I fell through the opening. I was trying to get a picture and tripped over my shoelace. I lost my shoe somewhere."

"It's up here," Benny said.

"Can you get out the door?" asked Henry. "We couldn't get it open from the outside."

"I tried it and couldn't get it open from the inside either," Todd said.

"We'll have to go down and figure out a way to help him," said Henry. He put his foot on the conveyor belt. "I think it's sturdy."

"I can go down," Jessie said. "I weigh less than Henry."

"Let's use the rope that Depla is tied up with," said Henry. "Maybe we can use it to help you down."

The children went outside and removed Depla's

rope. "I don't think it is going to be long enough," said Jessie. "And I don't want Depla to wander off."

"Over there!" said Benny.

On the ground outside the cannery was a pile of rope. "I didn't see this when we came in," Henry said, picking up the rope.

"Maybe the elves left it!" said Benny. "It's like the story of the boy who needed help rounding up his sheep!"

Henry pulled on the rope. "Well, wherever it came from, it's just what we needed."

Back inside, they tied a loop at the end and lowered Jessie down the conveyer. "It's safe," she called back up. "It didn't move at all."

Todd was pale, and he was holding his right arm. His camera lay next to him. "My camera might be broken too."

"Do you think you can climb up with one hand if Henry and Dr. Iris pull with this rope?" Jessie asked, untying the rope around her waist.

"I think so," Todd said.

Jessie picked up the camera and slung it over her shoulder. Slowly, they made their way back up the conveyor belt to safety.

When they got outside, they helped Todd onto Depla. "We need to get back quickly," said Henry. "The ashfall from the volcano is blowing this way."

Benny pointed at the sky. In the distance, there was a dark cloud that looked like the one they had seen from the airplane. "Really quickly!" he added.

CHAPTER 10

NOT HOME YET

I'll radio for a boat to come get us," Gunnar said when they returned to the house.

"But what about the horses?" Violet asked.

Gunnar looked very serious. "That is a problem. I don't want to leave them here. We need to get them back to the stable, so they'll be protected from the ash. We can't put them on the boat."

"We can take the horses back while you and Todd wait for the boat," Henry said.

114

Gunnar looked at Dr. Iris. "What do you think?"

"I think it's the best solution," she said. "We don't have many choices. If we leave soon, we can be back at the farmhouse by late afternoon."

When they went to saddle the horses, the animals were restless, as if they knew something was wrong.

"Hafli and Depla would most likely just follow along to stay with the others," Gunnar said, "but it's still best to attach a rope and lead them. Jessie, why don't you take Depla. Your horse and Depla like each other, so you shouldn't have any trouble leading.

"Violet, all the horses like Lappi, so do you think you can go first and lead Hafli? Dr. Iris can call out directions."

"Yes," Violet said. She patted her horse on the neck. "Lappi and I can do it. I think we both want to get back to the guesthouse before anything else goes wrong."

Hafli seemed confused why they were leaving Gunnar behind. He didn't want to move at first, but Violet urged him on until he started to follow along.

As they rode, they could see the sky to the west getting darker. "There is a bad smell in the air," Jessie said.

"When volcanoes erupt, they let off a sulfur smell," Dr. Iris said.

The horses were mostly calm, except Henry's seemed a little jittery, moving from side to side and turning his head to look around.

"It's okay," Henry said, patting him. "We'll be back soon."

The ride seemed to take longer than it had the day before, and by the time they reached the guesthouse, Gunnar had already arrived.

"We didn't know you'd get back before us," Jessie said.

"It's a long way by land, but it's just a short distance by water," he explained. "Todd is at a doctor's office. We should get a call soon about how he is doing. The boat ride was a bit rough, and he wasn't feeling well by the time we got back."

The Aldens helped put the horses in their stalls.

A gray cat came out. The cat went up to Kisi, and the horse lowered its head. The cat rubbed against Kisi's nose.

"Kisi's cat has been worried too," Gunnar said.

When they were finished, they went back to the guesthouse, and Dr. Iris told them what she had decided to do. "I'm afraid we are going to have to leave Iceland a little bit early," she said. "I'll try to get us on a flight tomorrow. We'll get up early and drive back south."

"I'm ready to get out of here," a voice said from the doorway. It was Todd. His arm was bandaged, and he had a bruise on his face. "The arm isn't broken, but I think I should take it easy for a while, so a nice long plane ride sounds like just the thing for me."

"Here's your camera," said Jessie, picking it up off the table. "I'm afraid it is broken."

Todd sighed and took the camera from Jessie. He opened up the camera bag to put it inside, but the rock from their first day was inside. He quickly closed the bag's flap.

Violet decided to speak up. "Todd, maybe you should put that rock back," she said. "If you take it with you and it's an elf rock, more things will go wrong."

"Yes," Benny said. "You'll make the elves really mad if you put them on an airplane."

"What's all this?" Dr. Iris asked.

Violet explained about all of the things that had gone wrong on the trip and how it reminded her of the story of the elf rock.

When she was done, Todd shook his head. "There are good explanations for the things that have gone wrong. Our tire blew out because we hit a rock. I tripped and fell because my shoe was untied."

"You do, do that a lot," said Benny.

Todd frowned.

Dr. Iris cleared her throat. "No matter what has been causing our bad luck," she said, "I do think you should return the rock. I'm not sure what the law is in Iceland about taking stones and other natural items."

"It's only a rock!" Todd said. "No one will miss it."

Dr. Iris sighed. "That's not the point. We should put it back."

The next morning, they said good-bye to Helga and Gunnar and the horses.

"We're taking a different route back," Dr. Iris said, "on a major roadway, so we shouldn't have any unexpected car mishaps."

"Good!" Violet said.

In a few hours, they were back at the gas station. Dr. Iris pulled in and parked the car.

Henry looked out over the area. "There are a lot of rock formations. Are you sure you can find the right spot?" he asked Todd.

"Yes, I remember," Todd grumbled. "But I still think this is silly. There are rocks everywhere here." He looked down at his cast. "Then again, maybe it is for the best."

"Can I carry it?" Benny asked.

"Sure," Todd said.

Todd got the rock and led the way out into the

field. "It was about here," he said, pointing down to the ground.

"Are you sure?" Violet asked.

"There's an indentation in the ground," Todd said. "I'm sure."

Benny set it down very carefully. "Good-bye, elves, if you are in there," he said. "I'm sorry we took you on our trip without asking if you wanted to go."

They got back in the car. "Our flight isn't for a couple of hours, so I've planned a treat for us before we leave," Dr. Iris said. "We're going to the famous Blue Lagoon to soak in the water. It will be a nice way to relax. Plus, we have a lot to talk about!"

They could see steam rising from the water even before they reached the lagoon. After they showered and put on their swimsuits, they met at the steps that led down into the water.

"I've never seen water so blue," Jessie said.

"It looks magical," added Violet.

The Aldens waded into the warm water. As they were relaxing, Dr. Iris said, "I need to send a message

once we get to the airport about what we think we might put in the program. What do you kids think?"

The children were quiet for a moment. Then Jessie spoke up. "We didn't find any solid proof that elves exist. But lots of bad things did happen—things that make it easy to believe that the stories about elves could be true."

"Not just bad things either," said Violet. She told Dr. Iris about the horse that led them out of the rock maze and the rope they had found when they needed it most.

"We also learned that the landscape can change the way legends are told," said Henry. "And while I'm not sure if elves or trolls exist, I know that living here can make it easier to believe."

Dr. Iris nodded. "That sounds like just the right ending for the show."

As the children soaked, Violet swirled her hand through the water. "Water like this seems so magical," she said. "It seems like a magical creature should live here."

"Funny you should mention sea creatures." A big smile appeared on Dr. Iris's face.

"Why?" Benny asked.

"Because I think there is another legend we should check out," said Dr. Iris.

"Where are we going?" asked Henry.

"To another island," said Dr. Iris. "But this time, one that is much warmer."

Read on for a sneak preview of

MERMAIDS OF THE DEEP BLUE SEA

the third book in the all-new
Boxcar Children Creatures of
Legend series!

"So what brings you to Puerto Rico?" the flight attendant asked. "Are you visiting family?"

The young woman led the four children down the aisle of the airplane. Henry Alden was in the front of the line. But it was his little brother, Benny, who spoke first. "We're searching for sea monsters!" Benny said.

The flight attendant chuckled. She turned around to look at the youngest Alden. "Is that so?"

"We really are!" Benny held up two of his carry-on items, a toy shark and a toy alligator. He pretended one was chasing the other.

The flight attendant gave Benny a friendly smile. "It looks like you've already found two right there."

Benny shook his head. "These are sea *animals*. We're looking for sea *monsters*."

Henry ruffled Benny's hair. At fourteen, he was used to his six-year-old brother's excitement. "I think what he means is, we're visiting a friend of our grandfather's. She's like family."

Benny stopped and looked up from his toys for a

moment. "Oh yeah. We're doing that too!"

The flight attendant smiled. "Well, this works out perfectly!" She stopped at a row where a girl was sitting. The girl's hair was tied in purple ribbons, and she had a purple stuffed animal on her lap. "This is Katharine. She's visiting family too—her grandfather. And she's ten, just like you, Violet. We've arranged to seat you all together for the flight."

"Hi," said Violet. "I like your outfit. Purple is my favorite color." Violet turned to her older sister, Jessie. "I'll give up my turn to sit by the window and sit by Katharine instead. Benny can have the window seat."

"Yay!" Benny cheered. "Maybe I'll spot a shipwreck or a giant sea monster!"

Before long, the plane was in the air, and Katharine turned to Violet. "Is it true what your little brother said? Are you really going to look for sea monsters?"

"Benny can be a little bit…dramatic," Violet said. She looked over at her brother. He had taken out a plastic octopus and was making whooshing sounds with his cheeks as it swam through the air.

"We're helping our grandfather's friend," Violet said. "She's doing a television show for kids. It's about creatures that people have told stories about for a long time. We're helping her investigate."

"Wow, that sounds amazing," said Katharine. "What kinds of creatures?"

Benny leaned around Violet. "First, we learned about bigfoots in Colorado. Then, in Iceland, we looked for elves and trolls. Now—sea monsters!"

"We don't know exactly what we'll be looking for at this stop," Violet explained. "Just that it has to do with the water."

"Does your grandfather live in Puerto Rico?" Jessie asked Katharine.

Katharine shook her head. "He's writing a book that takes place there. He rented a big boat. We're going to stay on it while he does research."

"You get to sleep on a boat?" Benny asked. "I hope we can do that."

"What kind of books does he write?" Henry

asked from across the aisle.

"Exciting ones! Are you going to learn about luscas too? My grandfather is putting one of those in his book."

"What's that?" Benny asked.

Katharine shuddered. "They are terrible creatures that come out of the water and wrap their tentacles around you." She hugged her stuffed animal close.

Benny's eyes grew wider. "Really?"

Katharine nodded. "Some are so big, their tentacles can wrap around boats and sink them. I wish I had some paper. I could draw you a picture."

Violet took out a notepad and a pencil case from her backpack. "Here you go."

"I've heard of luscas before," Jessie said. "We didn't get to that one yet, Benny, but it's in my book of legends." Jessie was twelve. She had been busy the last few days answering Benny's many questions about creatures from the sea.

"Luscas aren't just a legend," Katharine said as she started to draw. "I've read about them on the internet." She drew a creature that had a shark's head and a body like an octopus with too many tentacles. "There are lots of websites about it."

"Some things on the internet aren't true," Jessie said.

"You check them out. You'll see." The girl added in some sharp teeth to the creature's mouth. She held up the drawing. "Isn't it scary?"

Benny looked closely at the drawing. He had been excited to learn about the legends of the sea. And he didn't mind sharks or octopuses. But seeing the two of them together, with extralong tentacles and sharp teeth, was a different story.

"On second thought, maybe I don't want to stay on a boat after all."

THE BOXCAR CHILDREN®

GREAT ADVENTURE

An Exciting 5-Book Miniseries

**Henry, Jessie, Violet, and Benny Alden
are on a secret mission that takes
them around the world!**

When Violet finds a turtle statue that nobody's seen before in an old trunk at home, the children are on the case! The clue turns out to be an invitation to the Reddimus Society, a secret guild dedicated to returning lost treasures to where they belong.

Now the Aldens must take the statue and six mysterious boxes across the country to deliver them safely—and keep them out of the hands of the Reddimus Society's enemies. It's just the beginning of the Boxcar Children's most amazing adventure yet!

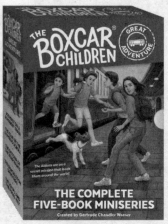

Check out The Boxcar Children® Interactive Mysteries!

Have you ever wanted to help the Aldens crack a case? Now you can with these interactive, choose-your-own-path-style mysteries!

978-0-8075-2850-1 · US $6.99

978-0-8075-2860-0 · US $6.99

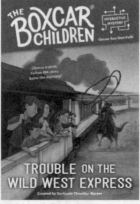

978-0-8075-2862-4 · US $6.99

Look out for
The Boxcar Children® DVDs!

The Boxcar Children and *Surprise Island* animated movie adaptations are both available on DVD, featuring Martin Sheen and J.K. Simmons.

Introducing The Boxcar Children®
Educational Augmented Reality App!

Watch and listen to your favorite Alden characters as they spring from the pages to act out scenes, ask questions, and encourage a love of reading. The app works with any paperback or hardcover copy of *The Boxcar Children*, the first book in the series, printed after 1942.

Add to Your
Boxcar Children Collection!

The first sixteen books are now available in
four individual boxed sets!

978-0-8075-0854-1 · US $24.99

978-0-8075-0857-2 · US $24.99

978-0-8075-0840-4 · US $24.99

978-0-8075-0834-3 · US $24.99

The Boxcar Children® Bookshelf includes the first twelve
books, a bookmark with complete title checklist,
and a poster with activities.

978-0-8075-0855-8 · US $69.99

THE BOXCAR CHILDREN
SURPRISE ISLAND
THE YELLOW HOUSE MYSTERY
MYSTERY RANCH
MIKE'S MYSTERY
BLUE BAY MYSTERY
THE WOODSHED MYSTERY
THE LIGHTHOUSE MYSTERY
MOUNTAIN TOP MYSTERY
SCHOOLHOUSE MYSTERY
CABOOSE MYSTERY
HOUSEBOAT MYSTERY
SNOWBOUND MYSTERY
TREE HOUSE MYSTERY
BICYCLE MYSTERY
MYSTERY IN THE SAND
MYSTERY BEHIND THE WALL
BUS STATION MYSTERY
BENNY UNCOVERS A MYSTERY
THE HAUNTED CABIN MYSTERY
THE DESERTED LIBRARY MYSTERY
THE ANIMAL SHELTER MYSTERY
THE OLD MOTEL MYSTERY
THE MYSTERY OF THE HIDDEN PAINTING
THE AMUSEMENT PARK MYSTERY
THE MYSTERY OF THE MIXED-UP ZOO
THE CAMP-OUT MYSTERY
THE MYSTERY GIRL
THE MYSTERY CRUISE
THE DISAPPEARING FRIEND MYSTERY
THE MYSTERY OF THE SINGING GHOST
THE MYSTERY IN THE SNOW
THE PIZZA MYSTERY
THE MYSTERY HORSE
THE MYSTERY AT THE DOG SHOW
THE CASTLE MYSTERY
THE MYSTERY OF THE LOST VILLAGE
THE MYSTERY ON THE ICE
THE MYSTERY OF THE PURPLE POOL
THE GHOST SHIP MYSTERY
THE MYSTERY IN WASHINGTON, DC
THE CANOE TRIP MYSTERY
THE MYSTERY OF THE HIDDEN BEACH
THE MYSTERY OF THE MISSING CAT
THE MYSTERY AT SNOWFLAKE INN

THE MYSTERY ON STAGE
THE DINOSAUR MYSTERY
THE MYSTERY OF THE STOLEN MUSIC
THE MYSTERY AT THE BALL PARK
THE CHOCOLATE SUNDAE MYSTERY
THE MYSTERY OF THE HOT AIR BALLOON
THE MYSTERY BOOKSTORE
THE PILGRIM VILLAGE MYSTERY
THE MYSTERY OF THE STOLEN BOXCAR
THE MYSTERY IN THE CAVE
THE MYSTERY ON THE TRAIN
THE MYSTERY AT THE FAIR
THE MYSTERY OF THE LOST MINE
THE GUIDE DOG MYSTERY
THE HURRICANE MYSTERY
THE PET SHOP MYSTERY
THE MYSTERY OF THE SECRET MESSAGE
THE FIREHOUSE MYSTERY
THE MYSTERY IN SAN FRANCISCO
THE NIAGARA FALLS MYSTERY
THE MYSTERY AT THE ALAMO
THE OUTER SPACE MYSTERY
THE SOCCER MYSTERY
THE MYSTERY IN THE OLD ATTIC
THE GROWLING BEAR MYSTERY
THE MYSTERY OF THE LAKE MONSTER
THE MYSTERY AT PEACOCK HALL
THE WINDY CITY MYSTERY
THE BLACK PEARL MYSTERY
THE CEREAL BOX MYSTERY
THE PANTHER MYSTERY
THE MYSTERY OF THE QUEEN'S JEWELS
THE STOLEN SWORD MYSTERY
THE BASKETBALL MYSTERY
THE MOVIE STAR MYSTERY
THE MYSTERY OF THE PIRATE'S MAP
THE GHOST TOWN MYSTERY
THE MYSTERY OF THE BLACK RAVEN
THE MYSTERY IN THE MALL
THE MYSTERY IN NEW YORK
THE GYMNASTICS MYSTERY
THE POISON FROG MYSTERY
THE MYSTERY OF THE EMPTY SAFE
THE HOME RUN MYSTERY
THE GREAT BICYCLE RACE MYSTERY

THE MYSTERY OF THE WILD PONIES
THE MYSTERY IN THE COMPUTER GAME
THE HONEYBEE MYSTERY
THE MYSTERY AT THE CROOKED HOUSE
THE HOCKEY MYSTERY
THE MYSTERY OF THE MIDNIGHT DOG
THE MYSTERY OF THE SCREECH OWL
THE SUMMER CAMP MYSTERY
THE COPYCAT MYSTERY
THE HAUNTED CLOCK TOWER MYSTERY
THE MYSTERY OF THE TIGER'S EYE
THE DISAPPEARING STAIRCASE MYSTERY
THE MYSTERY ON BLIZZARD MOUNTAIN
THE MYSTERY OF THE SPIDER'S CLUE
THE CANDY FACTORY MYSTERY
THE MYSTERY OF THE MUMMY'S CURSE
THE MYSTERY OF THE STAR RUBY
THE STUFFED BEAR MYSTERY
THE MYSTERY OF ALLIGATOR SWAMP
THE MYSTERY AT SKELETON POINT
THE TATTLETALE MYSTERY
THE COMIC BOOK MYSTERY
THE GREAT SHARK MYSTERY
THE ICE CREAM MYSTERY
THE MIDNIGHT MYSTERY
THE MYSTERY IN THE FORTUNE COOKIE
THE BLACK WIDOW SPIDER MYSTERY
THE RADIO MYSTERY
THE MYSTERY OF THE RUNAWAY GHOST
THE FINDERS KEEPERS MYSTERY
THE MYSTERY OF THE HAUNTED BOXCAR
THE CLUE IN THE CORN MAZE
THE GHOST OF THE CHATTERING BONES
THE SWORD OF THE SILVER KNIGHT
THE GAME STORE MYSTERY
THE MYSTERY OF THE ORPHAN TRAIN
THE VANISHING PASSENGER
THE GIANT YO-YO MYSTERY
THE CREATURE IN OGOPOGO LAKE
THE ROCK 'N' ROLL MYSTERY
THE SECRET OF THE MASK
THE SEATTLE PUZZLE
THE GHOST IN THE FIRST ROW
THE BOX THAT WATCH FOUND
A HORSE NAMED DRAGON

THE GREAT DETECTIVE RACE
THE GHOST AT THE DRIVE-IN MOVIE
THE MYSTERY OF THE TRAVELING TOMATOES
THE SPY GAME
THE DOG-GONE MYSTERY
THE VAMPIRE MYSTERY
SUPERSTAR WATCH
THE SPY IN THE BLEACHERS
THE AMAZING MYSTERY SHOW
THE PUMPKIN HEAD MYSTERY
THE CUPCAKE CAPER
THE CLUE IN THE RECYCLING BIN
MONKEY TROUBLE
THE ZOMBIE PROJECT
THE GREAT TURKEY HEIST
THE GARDEN THIEF
THE BOARDWALK MYSTERY
THE MYSTERY OF THE FALLEN TREASURE
THE RETURN OF THE GRAVEYARD GHOST
THE MYSTERY OF THE STOLEN SNOWBOARD
THE MYSTERY OF THE WILD WEST BANDIT
THE MYSTERY OF THE SOCCER SNITCH
THE MYSTERY OF THE GRINNING GARGOYLE
THE MYSTERY OF THE MISSING POP IDOL
THE MYSTERY OF THE STOLEN DINOSAUR BONES
THE MYSTERY AT THE CALGARY STAMPEDE
THE SLEEPY HOLLOW MYSTERY
THE LEGEND OF THE IRISH CASTLE
THE CELEBRITY CAT CAPER
HIDDEN IN THE HAUNTED SCHOOL
THE ELECTION DAY DILEMMA
THE DOUGHNUT WHODUNIT
THE ROBOT RANSOM
THE LEGEND OF THE HOWLING WEREWOLF
THE DAY OF THE DEAD MYSTERY
THE HUNDRED-YEAR MYSTERY
THE SEA TURTLE MYSTERY
SECRET ON THE THIRTEENTH FLOOR
THE POWER DOWN MYSTERY
MYSTERY AT CAMP SURVIVAL
THE MYSTERY OF THE FORGOTTEN FAMILY
NEW! THE SKELETON KEY MYSTERY
NEW! SCIENCE FAIR SABOTAGE

GERTRUDE CHANDLER WARNER discovered when she was teaching that many readers who like an exciting story could find no books that were both easy and fun to read. She decided to try to meet this need, and her first book, *The Boxcar Children*, quickly proved she had succeeded.

Miss Warner drew on her own experiences to write the mystery. As a child she spent hours watching trains go by on the tracks opposite her family home. She often dreamed about what it would be like to set up housekeeping in a caboose or freight car—the situation the Alden children find themselves in.

While the mystery element is central to each of Miss Warner's books, she never thought of them as strictly juvenile mysteries. She liked to stress the Aldens' independence and resourcefulness and their solid New England devotion to using up and making do. The Aldens go about most of their adventures with as little adult supervision as possible—something else that delights young readers.

Miss Warner lived in Putnam, Connecticut, until her death in 1979. During her lifetime, she received hundreds of letters from girls and boys telling her how much they liked her books.